Letters from Diaspora

Letters from Diaspora

Arnesa Buljusmic-
Kustura

For those who have been displaced by war and genocide; with souls that feel split between two lands.

Contents

Author's Note

Rabija

Jasmina

Safet

Aisa

Hana

Selma

Sabahudin

Ivana

Alma

Tarik

Vesna

Fatima

Footnotes

About Author

Acknowledgments

Author's Note

The portrayal of war that we see in media is often washed down as if war is just a simple game of cat and mouse. The truth about war is that it destroys everything; homes, lives, loves, innocence, beauty and not just buildings as the media portrayals of war would have us believe. On April 6, 1992 the war in Bosnia and Herzegovina broke out. That war resulted in the Siege of Sarajevo, the longest siege of a city in modern history, and multiple genocides of the Bosnian Muslim population throughout the country. While it has been 20 years since the war and genocide, the Bosnian population remains unhealed and too traumatized to speak publicly of the horrors they lived through between 1992 and 1995. But if you are lucky to know them, to love them, and to speak to them you will find that every once in a while the truth about their trauma slips out of their mouths. This book is about the Bosnian immigrants that survived the war and genocide. These stories, although fictionalized, are based of real people, real trauma, and real experiences. To all victims of war and genocide, I hope you find the courage to speak your truth even when your voice shakes and even when it hurts to remember. These 13 stories are just a handful of the many others that get left unspoken, I hope Letters from Diaspora serves as a catalyst for others to share their pain too. Let's be the ones to start the healing process.

There is a war inside my mouth

A Battle on my tongue

Between my mother language and this adopted one

The words struggle to get out

Fighting with one another

Constantly at odds with each other

The one that wins; is the one I write in

Letters from Diaspora

Rabija

My mother named me Rabija. In Arabic she said it was written as Rabiah and it meant springtime. I was born in the springtime and she found it appropriate. She used to tell me how the day I was born all of the flowers seemed to have suddenly blossomed as if they were waiting for my birth. It was the greatest day of her short life.

She died in the first months of the war, on my 15th birthday. Her death was painless. She died in her sleep. I mourned her for quite some time until I saw the destruction the war brought to the country she loved with all of her heart. I stopped mourning her when I realized how lucky she was to not have had to witness the sorrow of the people in our village, the grief the war brought to her neighbors, and the hate the oppressors brought their way as they moved from village to village murdering and ransacking those that did not share their religion.

It was also in the month of April that followed the end of the war that I decided to pack up my bags and leave the destruction that I now saw everywhere. I could not handle the fear that I saw, let alone the fear that I now felt.

I miss the way the fruit trees blossomed and their flowers covered the streets. I miss the smell of lilac that spread through the land. I miss the feeling of waking up in the morning and feeling at home. I miss a lot.

I miss my country, but I yearned for safety much more than I did for a home. I figured the country would still be there one day. I could always return to it.

The war ended. The country I loved was desolated by violence but it lived. It survived and so did we. Yet, we are still lost. Hopeless and traumatized. We are searching for something we aren't sure we know. We are afraid and yet we speak very little about the fear that we feel. I often wonder if my Bosnian friends do not speak about our past for fear it will repeat itself again.

Maybe it is the fact that if we open our mouths to speak about the past, we would find ourselves unable to ever stop. That is how pain works. Once it is recognized, it flows endlessly, it grows and grows until we simply cannot control it anymore.

Next month is April. The month I was born in, the month my mother died in, the month the war started, and the month I left the country my mother loved. It is somewhat poetic to me to return to the home I once loved for the first time in twenty years during this month. April was always beautiful in Bosnia and I wonder if it remained as such.

I dream of my return to the land of blossomed trees. I can already smell the lilacs.

I'm coming home.

Jasmina

In the summer of 1994 I lost my virginity on the cold basement ground of an eight floor building. You wouldn't think that was romantic but the two of us believed our days were up. What is more romantic than admitting your love right before your deaths? Isn't that at least what all the movies portray. The bombs over the grey and dreary sky sounded like fireworks in those moments. Nothing mattered. Not the possibility of death. Starvation. Nothing. It was just him and I, on the cold ground. He died several days after. I lived.

The tragedy is not that he died, but that I did not die with him. Oh, believe me, I thought about ending my life many times. I wanted to follow him to the depths of heaven or hell. It did not matter to me. I was in love. I was young. I was a coward. He was *a saheed*. A martyr. He died fighting to protect our home, our country, and the worst of it is that he died to protect me.

The last words he spoke to me echo in my head even 20 years later: "Jasmina, I will return to you. We'll be happy, Jasmina. It will all be over soon." I wanted to kill myself after his soldiers brought his body to my footsteps. I screamed for days, unafraid of the possibility of Serbs finding me. I wanted to dig the pain out of my body. I begged Allah to give me claws. I begged him to end me. I begged even that a bomb hits the building in which I laid with him for the first time.

I'm not ashamed of my begging. I am ashamed that Allah picked me to live. How could I live and Samir could not? What justice was there allowing me to live with this pain for the rest of my life? My heart still feels as if it breaking. 20 years later and I find my soul still burning. I curse the country that gave birth to me. I curse the people in it. I curse everything.

I never married. I have no children. My parents died in that war. I have a sister somewhere in Sweden I speak to once or twice a year. I left Bosnia in 2001 and I never returned. I refuse to. That land is cursed. I saw him everywhere and in everything years following his death. I saw his smile on every tram stop. I saw his tears on every park bench. I saw his stubbornness in every alley of Sarajevo. That city no longer belongs to me. That country he fought to protect spit me out as if I was just a bad taste in its mouth.

I cannot return home. I have no home here. I am split in between two places and neither one wants me any longer. I am too broken for both. One reminds me of him. The other tells me to forget him. I refuse them both. I keep him close to me. I let the pain of losing memories of him drive me to do better. Sometimes I fail. Most times I fail. I have not committed suicide yet. I am still figuring out if I have not followed him because I am brave or because I am coward.

Maybe it is a combination of both. My new home in this new country looks like a shrine to him. No wonder I never remarried. His roots took up a home in my heart, how do I pull them out after this much time? I begged Allah to give me strength to mourn him.

The thing is, I have not stopped praying. I am not sure if I even believe Allah listens any longer but the minute the clock strikes the right time; you will find me with my knees bent making *Salah*. I stopped praying he would bring Samir back. These days I pray for peace. I pray for patience. I pray my soul somehow finds itself healed. I'm sure God has bigger issues to deal with than the broken heart of a Bosnian woman but I pray nonetheless. It has become a habit, ingrained in me since Nana first taught me how to pray.

Nana died in that war too, along with everyone else. She was 80 years old at the time. Some would say that is a long enough of a life lived. Those people probably don't know how it feels to die burning alive in the home that gave birth to five generations, a home that gave birth to everything you ever loved. My grandmother gave birth to this land only to see it consume her in the end.

I saw them burn. I saw his body on the footsteps of the home I believe would hold our children one day. Is twenty years enough time to get over that?

How can I get over that?

Twenty years and I still see their faces. Twenty years of peace everywhere except my own head, my heart, my reality. How am I complaining though? I survived at least. Here I am, in the greatest country in the world. A land full of possibilities and I am still spilling tears over people that were laid to rest twenty years ago.

How much more of a fool could I get? I never knew how to appreciate anything that was given to me. Not even survival.

Instead, I am here. I am mourning his death twenty years later. I am mourning their deaths. Sometimes I feel as if I died that day too. I'm alive. I'm alive. Thank Allah I am alive. My guilt is the punishment for my survival but at least I survived.

Safet

When I was five years old my grandfather took me to the mosque for the first time. We practiced praying for a while before I got the hang of it and now it was finally time to pray in a mosque. My best friend at the time was named Milan. That same day his grandfather took him to the church across the mosque. We both prayed in our individual holy houses and afterwards our grandfathers played chess together while we ate ice cream in front of the only café in the town.

It became a routine for us. First prayer, then chess and then ice cream. As we grew our grandfathers taught us how to play chess too. This was our Friday tradition for seven years. Even as we became interested in girls and chasing after them we kept up our Fridays and our prayers. Those were the best days of my life.

In March of 1992, we had our last Friday prayer and chess game. Milan told me his father was getting ready to leave this town and I asked him where he would go. It was then he told he would be joining his Serb brothers in taking up arms. He said he was fighting for the land that belonged to the Serbs and that we couldn't play chess together anymore.

Even our grandfathers were quiet that day. They said little as they played their chess game. It was mine that spoke up first. He said, "Here we are playing a simple game of chess and those politicians over there are doing the same, just with our lives as the pawns."

The fighting started a few weeks after our last game. It was Milan's father that knocked our door and told us to get out. He said our land belonged to the Serbs now and that us Muslim had no business being there. I remembered Milan's father as a kind and intellectual man. He had glasses, a strong chin, and eyes that were soft. He had a quiet voice too, but that was all before the war. He had a beard now and a menacing look on his face. His eyes were not soft but rather filled with hate.

I asked him where his son was and he said that Muslim dogs such as me shouldn't worry about Serbs and what they do. They split the men and women up and told us to start walking. In a matter of days, we were all holed up in what used to be a hotel. Every day, they'd take men out of what they call the camp and the men never returned. I used to just wait to be taken to my death just as the rest of them were. My grandfather was among those men. We still have not found his remains.

I never saw Milan's father again after the camp got freed but I did see Milan. It was last year when I went to visit my hometown. The mosque I used to pray in with my grandfather was rebuilt after being destroyed in the war. I went to pray and Milan was standing outside of it, heading towards the church across from the mosque.

We stared at each other and I wondered who will speak first. I thought Milan would be ashamed to speak to the man whose grandfather was killed at the hands of his father, but he wasn't. He came up to me and hugged me instead, said how nice it was to see that I was alive and that he heard I lived in America now. I expected an apology, condolences on the death of my family members. Milan did not mention his father, just that his grandfather passed away a few years back. He had the privilege of growing old. He said how they still played chess every Friday even after we left.

He talked and I listened. I wanted to yell at him and make him apologize. I wanted to throw the pieces of chess in his face. I wanted to tell him that Muslim dogs such as myself shouldn't speak to him. I didn't. Instead, I simply listened to him and played a game of chess.

Milan's father still teaches at the local school. Milan works in the old factory. Their lives are the same as they would have been had it not been for the war and mine is destroyed.

I'm away from the home that used to be mine. The house I once lived in now belongs to a Serb family. The mosque I used to pray in has five members in it. I still haven't buried my grandfather. The café that I used to eat ice cream in front of no longer allows Muslims in it. The graves around the town I spent my childhood in are filled with bones of Muslim men and women who were killed just because they were Muslim.

The day I saw Milan was the day I vowed never to return to Bosnia again. There was nothing there for me anymore. Not a house, not a mosque, not a family, and not even a friend.

My wife gave birth to a boy this year. I named him after my grandfather. I named him Husein. One day I will teach him to play chess. We'll go to the mosque in this town instead and I'll even buy him ice cream. He'll have friends and I will too. I'll tell him how even the strongest of friendships get broken by war. I'll tell him stories of Milan and me, our grandfathers and their chess games, and the war that took everything from me.

Husein won't understand. He'll tell me I am being hateful, I'm sure. He'll tell me, just as they all do, to forgive and forget. And it's okay because it's only those that do not go through the hell of war that are able to forgive those responsible for it. At least I will know that Husein will not see war.

Aisa

The other day I made coffee for the two of us. Of course, you were nowhere near me so I drank the coffee by myself. Your cup was untouched. But in my mind, I pictured you across from me. For a few minutes, it was as if I could see your stern face, the lines drawn all over it, and your eyes glistening with the strength only you held. It was a sad day, mama. Most days here are sad. I know that when I call you I tell you everything is fine. The truth is that I lie, mama. I lie to you every time we speak. I tell myself the lies are for your own protection. You have enough to worry about without listening of my own sorrow. If I tell you I am fine, maybe it will bring some peace to your mind.

But back to the coffee. I drank it slowly, just like we used to. The aroma of it filled the room. It was as

if I was home with you. Do you want
to know what I said to you, mama? I
told you the truth. It was freeing. I
am unhappy, mama. In this country
and with him. Neither he nor this
country have the soul of Bosnia. My
days are spent alone. I work and I
come home. He and I barely speak. I
know he can sense my unhappiness.
It doesn't matter of course. Sorrow
and pain are the things I have gotten
accustomed to carrying on my back.
I miss you, mama. I cut our
telephone conversations short
because I can't bear to hear you
holding back your tears. I hold mine
back too.

It's been 5 years since I last saw your
face, since I held your hand, and
since I felt your touch. 5 long years.
We have a house now and we both
have good jobs, *Alhamdulillah*. Allah
has been good to us. But I don't have
you. What daughter can survive this
country without her mother. I try and
stay strong. After all, my strength is
the only thing I got from you. My
face, my body, and even my
movements belong to babo. But it's
the strength that matters the most,
mama and that is the greatest gift
you gave me. I pray to Allah that he
reunites us. I pray any chance I get.
Some days I wonder if Allah can
hear me. Are my prayers drowned

out by those who have it much worse than me? Whose lives are filled with much more misery than mine is?

Mama, I'd give the house, the cars, and everything on this green Earth for just a day spent drinking coffee with you. Real coffee. But real, Bosnian *kahva*. With *kocka*, of course. What is coffee without a sugar cube to go with it? We'd drink the coffee the way we always do, slowly and patiently. You'd tell me about how Fatima is having problems with her cows again and I'd listen as if you were reciting the greatest novel this world has been given. I'd fill your brain with my nonsense about which city I want to travel to and you'd listen and tell me in that soft voice of yours:

"*Inshallah, Kceri moja, InshAllah.*

What is a child when their parent is so far away? I miss you, mama. I swear some nights I can hear the sound of my heart breaking. I wonder if you can hear it too.

I miss you, mama.

Hana

My chest felt tight. My vision became dizzy. My body felt paralyzed although I knew I could move it. I couldn't breathe. Another panic attack.

They've lessened throughout the years but this time of the year they are always particularly bad. I closed my eyes and counted to 10. I tried to breathe. I tried not to remember but to no avail.

Cigarettes eased the aftermath of the panic attacks. My mother used to say nothing helped with stress like a good Bosnian cup of coffee and a cigarette to go with it. She swore by it all her life. I must say she was right. At least the memories of her come back when I have my *kahva* and *cigara*; and that always lessens the stress but the panic attacks were a different story.

Pictures of men spread in between my legs entered my thoughts like an uninvited guest. The memories came back. They always did. Alcohol did nothing to stop them, prayer rarely helped, and after several years of therapy I realized nothing would ever heal me. But I tried the breathing practice my doctors taught me and that lessened the pain.

I always felt tired after these panic attacks. Exhausted by something that happened to me 20 years ago. How silly it may have seemed to everyone in my life that a woman as successful as I am could be brought to her knees by a simple memory.

Tomorrow is the five-year anniversary of her death and the twentieth anniversary of mine. She died of cancer and I died at the hands of men fighting for nationalism. Physically I am alive. I'm healthy even, for the most part. But the day I was taken to the rape camp in Visegrad is the day I ceased to live.

I was only 14 years old at the time. "Fresh meat" the men said. "A pure grade a Muslim virgin" they'd laugh.

They showed me what it meant to be cruel at such a young age. They showed me what hate really does to humanity.

People tell me I won. All the stories would lead you to believe that I won over them. After all, I survived after so many did not. I made it out of the camp alive. I made my way to America. I got an education. I'm a doctor now. A woman that is a force to be reckoned with.

Yet, last year when I returned to my hometown, two of the men that forcibly took my body were in the line next to me. They were free. They were happy even. The lady at the register told me things have changed. People have moved on since the war. They all have to live together now. Is it really that I won? I got a Ph.D., sure, but what did they get? They got freedom after stealing everything that was mine. They got freedom after destroying everything that once made me a person.

Is that the kind of injustice I must live with? To know that the men that held me captive for a year, that abused me every day for a year, are able to go on and have happy lives? And what of me? I am successful, yet unable to sleep at night. I am free, yet imprisoned forever by the chains of my past. I am alive, yet barely human.

They tell me I should count my blessings. Many women had it worse than I did. Is that any sort of consolation? That some woman out there might have had it worse than my own torture? That she might have died at the hands of her oppressors? If I am supposed to feel lucky for staying alive with these memories that haunt me, then I must say people's concept of luck escape my understanding.

I am not lucky because I survived. Lucky would have been not having to be in a rape camp. Lucky would have been a childhood to call my own. Lucky would have been the ability to be as free as the girls in the rest of the world were. Lucky would have been a boy to crush on, a mark to buy ice cream with, and my parents to tuck me into bed at night.

Lucky would have been death over what I went through. An option that I considered many times after I came out of that rape camp.

I, however, was never brave enough to end my life. In many ways I was jealous of the women that were brave enough to do it. I realize that is something one is not supposed to admit, but it's the truth. People believe you to be strange but then again those people never were lucky enough to survive rape.

They don't have to live with the memories I do. Their bodies do not betray them when memories creep back in. They aren't stuck with the smell of war ingrained in their hair. They do not have to remember the men between their legs, thirsty and hungry and vicious in all the worst ways. They can watch fireworks and not scream. They can sleep through a thunderstorm instead of waking up, covered in sweat, believing you are back in the cross fire of the bombs that destroyed your villages, your houses, and most of all the people you once loved.

So, I guess I care very little about what people say and the things they think. Those who have never gone through war do not get to tell the rest of us how to deal with our pain, and the pain is immense. It never goes away. It didn't go away when I graduated from college, nor when I got my Master's degree, and it stayed with me even when I walked across the stage to get my PhD.

It's always there, just like the panic attacks. It's there when I cook, when I clean, when I am happy, and most of all when I am sad. I am often sad. I shouldn't be. I'm lucky. I survived.

Selma

There was a cold and overly professional voice on the other line. She said in accented English: "We believe we found your father's remains". She sounded British.

There was another mass grave that was dug up. They say they found hundreds of bones. It's been almost twenty years. I had to return to Bosnia to identify the belongings he was buried with. They said they didn't find all of the remains, just enough for him to be finally put to rest.

My entire life, I hoped that he was alive, somewhere, suffering from amnesia or something along those lines. I had hope. I wanted to know the truth all up until the moment I knew the truth. My father was dead. He was murdered. They say it must have happened in 1994.

I have to return to a home I barely even remember. I want to bury him next to our mother. My father died clutching the prayer beads his mother gave him before she left. There was a picture of me in his back pocket. I don't even have a picture of him; just bones.

He will be buried with a hundred others. Their families will mourn just as I will. They will cry just as I will. Yet, I feel my pain is worse than theirs.

My father was a hard man. He was not the friendly dad type you see on the television these days. He was harsh, cold, and continuously expecting more than he gave in return. But he was my father. He was the man that took me to my first dentist appointment and the man that held me when the first boy I ever loved told me he loved someone else. He was not perfect by any means, but he was my father and I loved him.

The autopsy determined he died by execution. His head was cut off from the rest of his body and his remains dug deep enough to hide the shame the country of Serbia should feel.

I went to law school after the war ended. I interned at The Hague. I saw the faces of those responsible for the deaths of my loved ones and one by one they gave them sentences that were too lenient, in my opinion. In some cases, they did not even give any sentences. I saw the faces of genocide and yet I could do very little to give them the punishment they deserved.

What is the punishment they deserve, you may ask? Can you tell me? How does one punish a genocide? Does death beget death? Do we truly believe in an "eye for an eye" theory? I'm not sure. Is evil punished by more evil? Is death punished by more death?

I'd say no but I am not brave enough to be honest. I only know I want my father back. I want my friends back. I want the life I never got to have back.

The year before the genocide started I was sitting in my tiny room and I was talking to my neighbor about the crush I had on the boy in our small town. We lived in Vlasenica. It wasn't a beautiful town by any means. It did not have the heart of Sarajevo, the soul of Mostar, nor the beauty of Pocitelj but it was the town

I was born in and just by that it meant everything to me. My father used to say it was not the architecture of the town that made it beautiful but rather the people. In his opinion, Vlasenica was a town of multiculturalism, a town where people always got along, where they loved each other. That is until the war broke out.

The day I returned to Vlasenica to burry my father the sky was clear and the sun was shining. To me it seemed as if the town I was born in was welcoming me back with open arms. I stood on top the hill above the town for a few hours, thinking about the life I could have led.

I thought of the memories I never got to make. This is what war does to people. It takes away everything even before they get to experience it.

It makes you bury a father 20 years after his death.

It makes you hate the home you once had.

Sabahudin/Sasa

Every once in a while when I close my eyes I can picture myself in front of my home in Bosnia. This feeling returns to me the most when the air seems to be the coldest. It's just a moment of peace but it's a moment I hold unto. I let it carry me throughout the day, if it wasn't for these moments I am unsure of how long I would have survived in America.

That home I picture has long been destroyed. When I tell my American friends about it they say I should not think of it; that I should be grateful I have a beautiful home here. It's true, I do have quite a beautiful home. There are people that spend a lifetime trying to purchase a home I did after such a short period of time. And yet…the material things can only make up for our heartbreak for so long. Eventually, the materialistic things we buy are no longer able to distract us from our own pain. The big house, the nice foreign car, the fancy clothing start to fade away when we start to remember the reason we are so focused on them.

I think to myself that if I buy enough nice things it will make up for the fact I lost so much at such a young age. I think that if I work hard enough, at least my future children will never go through what I did. But war doesn't pick and choose. One day everything could be taken from me again; it could be taken from my children too. I think that is what I fear the most.

These days the big house in the nice neighborhood doesn't do much for me. I leave it to go to work and I come home to find it empty. I think of the small house that was home to all nine of us in Bosnia. It was small, a two-bedroom home, and yet it fit all of us. It never felt tight or uncomfortable. It may have been the love within the home that gave us the comfort it did, rather than its structure. We never had very much growing up, but I can count the number of times I have laughed on one hand in America and in that small house, in the small village of a small country the laughs were uncountable. We had joy. The real sort of joy that carried you through the worst of the times. We had peace, if nothing else. My soul had peace.

I wish I could tell you that my soul has found peace in America too, but I would be lying. My days are spent working too many hours for people who turn their nose in disgust at my existence. My nights are worse. They are lonely and filled with memories, some I wish to forget.

The memories of war seem to creep in when I least expect them. All of a sudden, I find myself a scared boy again. Only now, I have no elder brothers to turn to for comfort. Not even my mother and father are there to hold me and tell me that everything will be okay and that we will survive. It's just me, hanging unto my sanity by a thread.

What a thin thread it actually is. Some nights are better than others. Some I am able to sleep. Some I am frozen in fear in a bed that is too large and too extravagant for a person like me. And there's this memory that often comes back to me whenever I lay in it:

My mother ran in to the house to let us know that Srebrenica has fallen to the Serbs. Through her tears she told us we must go now, that the entire village is fleeing. Through the war our parents tried to keep us brave. Babo would tell us to remain strong and my mother would tell us that Allah is watching over us. That day, they couldn't afford to keep lying to us. There was nothing in my mother's eyes other than fear. It was the sort of fear one had when they knew their last days were ahead of them. We packed a backpack each with what little belonging we had.

I still remember what I put in mine: an action figure, pants, a picture of my nana, a sandwich made of dandelions and honey, and a small Quran my grandfather gave me before he passed. Things I believed would make me strong. There is only so much strength a young boy can have in times of war.

With our backpacks we started to trek our way to safety. My older brothers made jokes on the way about the beautiful girls that awaited us in Tuzla. They were at that age where girls were their only priority. My youngest brother only cried, half out of fear and half out of hunger. My mother didn't say much, but I'd look over at her and see the prayers come out of her mouth. That was the last day I saw my family.

Somewhere along the way, the Serbs caught up to us. One by one, men were executed. My older brothers among them. My mother, despite the strong and fierce woman she was, buckled to her knees. I think the world could have heard her cries that day. I watched. Unable to do anything as the men were shot at. Those responsible for their deaths just simply laughed. I am unsure if they enjoyed the murders more or if was the pain they saw on the faces of us those of us they left to survive that truly brought them pleasure.

They executed Nihad last, he was only 17 years old and he was everyone's favorite. A kind soul, the people in our village would say he would be our imam one day. He loved Allah and because of his love for Allah he loved his people greatly. Never did he have a bad word to say to or about anyone. Light shined out of his eyes all up until the moment they held the pistol to his head. He turned to my mother then and said "Do not worry mama, Allah awaits me with open arms."

That was the moment that turned my mother into something I never saw before, a vengeful angel. She walked up quietly, came over to my youngest brother Sadik and me, and just gave us light kisses on the cheek. She looked at us with all the love in the world and said:

"Sasa, look after your brother and remember to pray."

And then as if she was an army herself, she charged the soldier that killed my brother and started to claw at his face. It didn't take long for one of the other soldiers to shoot her. She fell next to where my father was, where my brothers were, where our neighbors were. All of their blood creating one large puddle.

I think it was worth it to her, to show them that we had strength, that we would fight back even if it meant our deaths. My mother; born a warrior and died as one too.

They rounded up those of us they left alive; the women and the children and led us to Potocari. It was there I lost my youngest brother to the crowds of the hungry, scared, wounded Bosniaks. I still don't know if he survived or not.

I got lucky, I guess. Some translator felt sorry enough for me to keep me with her throughout the massacres. I survived somehow. Made it to a refugee camp, then an orphanage, and then somewhere in America with a Croatian family that wanted to adopt.

I've lived a good life here. I have a house now. A big house. It's huge. I have a woman that will one day be my wife. Maybe, one day when I let go of the fear I have I'll have kids too. But the house is the most important. The big, nice house in a nice and safe neighborhood. The house I have nightmares in. The beautiful house I worked so hard for, a home that is supposed to be a safe haven from my past.

Yet whenever I close my eyes in it, I am right back where I started. A sad, scared little boy who lost his family and his home.

Ivana

"He is a good man"-my mama said to me the night before our wedding. "The kind of man that will take care of you"- she smiled at me.

It was a beautiful wedding and he really was a good man. A hafiz of the Quran. His father was an imam. He was kind, which mattered most of all. He was the sort of the man that would give the shirt off his back to a complete stranger.

When the war broke out, he tried as much as he could to save as many as he could. He'd call friends in Croatia and Serbia, asking them to house the people from his *mahala*. If he could have he would have evacuated the entire city of Sarajevo, and he still would have stayed behind. He was a pure soul, gentle and lovely.

When the first shelling campaign started to hit Sarajevo, he held my hand and sang me my favorite song. He promised that I would survive the war, that he would find a way to keep me safe.

And he did. It was in December of 1993 that he found someone who was willing to smuggle me out of Sarajevo and into Belgrade. He sold the gold ducats his family had for decades just to pay to get me out of the war zone. But he decided to stay behind. Belgrade was not safe for a Bosniak and I was at least half a Serb.

The night before I left, we cried together in our bed, in the home I believed we would have lived in forever. When we fell in love, our religion did not matter. I was a Christian and he was a Muslim and yet we believed we could last forever. We probably would have had it not been for the war. Suddenly the fact I was a Christian and he a Muslim mattered much more than before.

I was never religious. My family barely celebrated Christmas and never observed Ramadan, they were communists after all. Hasan came from a long line of one of Sarajevo's finest Muslim families. He prayed five times a day and read the Quran whenever he could. I found beauty in the way he loved God. It was breathtaking to me, to see a person with so much hope for this world.

It's strange, you know? To love someone who is your complete opposite. While I partied and danced all night, he would recite Surah's from the Quran. It was chance that brought us together. My friend, Meliha, she wanted me to come to mosque with her for Ramadan and so I did. I saw him there; his voice was beautiful. He was reciting something from the Quran to the congregation. I fell in love instantly. We locked eyes and for the rest of the night we'd sneak looks at one another.

It's funny because he thought I was a Muslim. I had a hijab on and all. When I said my name was Kristina, he asked why my parents gave me a Christian name until Meliha said it was because I was a mixed. No matter the possible objections that we knew would come our way, we went out to coffee the next day and then a year later we got married. It was only six months of happiness I had within our marriage and then the war broke out.

I stayed in Belgrade for two years. I kept hoping the war would end and I would be able to return to my home and my husband. I survived Belgrade because I thought of our future together. I pictured us in our *mahala* of *Bistrik*, and our children running amok in our little *avlija*. I gave them names too, good Muslim names, ones that he would like. I even started to pray every night. I read the Quran so much I feel I almost have it memorized.

The war did end one day. I never returned to my home. I never saw my husband again. They say a sniper shot him down somewhere near or in Dobrinja. What he was doing over there, I'll never know. I figured he probably was trying to save someone or something. That's the kind of man he was, after all.

After the war ended I went to Vienna. I never wrote to my friends, to his family, nor to my own. After I got that phone call from Meliha letting me know of Muhamed's death, I was never quite the same. I'd wander around the streets of Vienna for hours, picturing our Sarajevo and yet not being brave enough to return to it.

I never went to Muhamed's funeral and I never saw his grave either. I couldn't. I'm sure his family had words to say about the wife that left and never looked back. But they didn't know. They couldn't have. They didn't realize the emptiness inside me after Muhamed's death. They didn't know of the nights I spent crying or the hours I prayed to God that he would bring me back to him.

They didn't even know I converted to Islam. I wonder if they saw me now, would they even recognize me? I feel I'm just a shell of a woman I once was.

I never remarried. I didn't even want children. He was the only man I ever loved and that love was enough for me.

People in this town, they too look down on me. They say "what a sad woman". They say I am wasting my life away, that I should marry and find myself a man. I forgive them for their unkind words. After all, they don't understand.

I could have married, but I chose God. I chose to pray and give myself to the Almighty. I chose to memorialize Muhamed in the best way that I could; I chose Islam and all the beauty it offered. While everyone felt sorry for me, the sad and lonely woman, I didn't. I had Allah, after all, and memories of my lost love. I am richer than they could ever be.

I am alive but most of all at one point in time I was loved and I loved, greatly and honestly. To me that is worth all the pain this *dunya* brings to us.

Alma

I'm not much for parties. I used to be. There were times I danced all night, where I sang right up until the dawn break. Things change, I suppose. People change and so do the parties they throw.

My friend is getting married in a few weeks. She had an engagement party, a bridal shower, and she will have a rehearsal dinner along with her bachelorette party too. The fact that there are so many different parties to celebrate one event is strange to me but I go to the parties anyway.

There's baby showers and bridal showers, engagement parties and wedding parties, there's anniversary parties and birthday parties, on top of all the holiday parties too. Where I come from there was never that many parties, or at least not as many reasons to celebrate. Just that there was always a time for dancing and singing.

The night before your wedding, you'd have a "girls' night". You'd listen to advice from your aunties, cousins, and friends. You'd make jokes about the wedding night while music played in the background and laughter filled the house. You'd put henna on your hands and think of the journey that awaited you. These parties were always small, intimate, and the sort of send of I would have personally preferred.

Weddings were always an ordeal back home. A party that'd last a couple days, instead of hours. They never consisted of perfectly picked out playlists, but rather local musicians that sang the songs people shelled out money for. The food was always homemade instead of served on a silver platter with the perfect garnish. And there was no need for glamour decorations when everything was already beautiful.

It's not that I mind American parties. It's just that they're so carefully planned out, I wonder if anyone actually has fun at them, especially the hosts. It's all far too prim and proper for my taste. A good party should have three things to be successful: food that fills you up, music that makes you feel, and friends that will never tire of dancing with you. All the rest of the stuff; the decorations, hors d'oeuvres and the fluff are unimportant.

I don't remember the last party I went to where I genuinely laughed. After the war broke out, there was no time for laughter, much less dancing and singing. But it must have been some time before the war; it may have been Hana's wedding or Zeljka's birthday party. One of the two. I think I danced till my feet bled, but then again I usually did.

It's interesting that we think of the small details about our pasts when nostalgia hits us. For example, if I wasn't so focused on my past in Bosnia, maybe I'd able to dance till my feet bled in America too. But instead, I chose to keep my dancing for the country that I used to call home. I guess that's why I'm not much for parties. It's hard to enjoy a party here when I'd rather be back there.

I have lived in this town for 18 years now. Each year I get adjusted to it more. I assimilate more. I've lost the accent I once had that identified me as foreign. My clothes, the highlights in my hair, and even my demeanor tell you that I, too, am an American. Almost everything shows how well adjusted I have become to this town and this country especially.

Everything except the parties, the music, and my refusal to dance. I have a party to go to tonight. I doubt I will dance. I certainly know I will not laugh. The food will be okay, the people will be nice, and the music will be loud and still I will yearn for the way we celebrated back home. It won't be a terrible time. I'll be cordial, witty, and charming. I'll give my present, I'll eat the food, and I'll even have a glass of wine. To anyone staring at me I will look as if I had a wonderful time.

But in my thoughts I'll think of the way I sang "*Sto te nema*" throughout the streets of Mostar at 2 am one night, how I danced *kolo* with my aunts only hours before, and how Zeljka and Samir laughed along with me the entire time.

After the party I will go home and I will take off my shoes, put on my coffee, and turn on my stereo. I'll put in my favorite cd and I'll simply listen.

I won't dance but I'll close my eyes and I'll send my mind back in time to the days I used to dance all night, until my feet bled. To the days, I sang my songs.

"Sto te nema, sto te nema

Kad na mlado poljsko cvjece

Biser nize ponoc nijema,

Kroz grudi mi zelja lijece

Sto te nema, sto te nema"

Tarik

I woke up this morning in a puddle of my own sweat. My hands were clutching the bed. I had nightmares again. No surprise there. My nightmares never stopped.

I got up from the bed and walked over to the stereo. I turned on the only thing that could me down. My mother's favorite song *"Zapklala secer Dula"* I found the song calming. It was an old Bosnian song. One from the *sevdah* variety.

It is a sad song, to some heartbreaking even but it always had a calming effect on me. The song is about a girl crying over a boy she loves to return from the war and the boy cursing the tsar for giving him an army to command. It ends with the boy telling the girl to marry someone else, that he was been caught by the enemy and forever separated from the woman he loved.

I loved a woman once too. She was a beauty. All the men in our *mahala* loved her and all the mothers wanted her to be their daughter in love. She was lovely with big brown eyes and long raven hair. She had a smile that lit up a room and her laugh was better than any *sevdalinka* this side of the world produced. She loved me too. We'd secretly meet behind the old well and talk about the books we read, the places we wanted to see and the songs that we loved. Her name was Amila. Amila Agic. Her favorite book was The Fortress. Her favorite song was *"Karanfile cvijece moje"*. She had a lot of favorites but the thing she loved most in the world was having me read to her behind the old well.

When the war broke out, I took up arms to defend the land that we both grew up in. I wanted to protect her. She promised that she would wait for me to return from the front lines and I promised that I would marry her as soon as this hell was over with. I told her that I would return soon and that we would sit behind the old well and

I'd rather her any story she wanted to listen to.

She said that it was never about the stories but about my voice. She kissed me then; it was the kind of kiss that was worth fighting any war for. The next morning, I took off to join the army. I was just a foolish boy, not knowing what it meant to be at war. They gave me an old barely working gun, a hand grenade, and told me to follow them.

Supplies were low and the city was under siege anyway. In just the first week on the front lines, I saw five of my friends die at the hands of the enemy. It made me sad but it never made me fear. I had Amila to think about. She kept me strong. The thought of waking up to her each morning kept me alive. It kept me sane throughout all the evil around me.

It didn't take long for our unit to be captured by the enemy. We were whisked off to the death camps just weeks after I took up arms. We were starved. We were beaten. We were tortured. We were eventually killed and disposed of.

I worried, of course. Every day I was certain I was going to my death but then I'd picture Amila. I'd see her bright smile, her pink cheeks, and raven hair and hope would return to my heart. I had hope. I'd remember the kiss. There was life to be had after this hell passed and I knew that one day it would pass. Just as all other wars passed before it.

The couple hundred men that were left alive, myself included, were rescued eventually. We survived, somehow. I knew the hell was going to pass.

After the camps, my body was just bones. I was hungry and tired but I still had hope. The war was going to come to an end soon. I could feel it in the air. There was hope.

Even as a boy at war I was still hopelessly naïve.

The war didn't end for another three years. By the time I returned to my *mahala*, almost nobody I once knew even lived there. Most of the houses were wrecked by grenades. The green fields around them filled with mines. People had to flee to the city where it was safe. I didn't find Amila in our *mahala* so I followed and went to city hoping I'd find someone that had news of her.

They did. They had news.

They said that she was killed by one of the grenades. They looked at me with pity and sorrow as they said those words.

"Amila is dead, I am sorry".

People gathered and hugged me. They spoke their condolences and said their prayers.

As for me? I was lost. I cried. Men aren't supposed to cry, not even in times of war. Maybe especially not in times of war but I cried. I yelled. I screamed. I drank myself into a stupor.

I had hope. I believed that the hell would pass. I was wrong.

I mourned her death for what seemed like an eternity. Long after the war was finished I thought about us behind that old well. I pictured her raven hair and that smile that lit up the world.

Anytime, I go back to Bosnia, I visit her grave. I talk to her just as if it she was here. I hope she hears me. I hope she know I still love her, even after all these years.

As for me, I have my nightmares and the *sevdah* to calm them down with. I wake every morning exhausted by the night before. Piercing screams of people in the camps, sounds of grenades over the city, and the smell of death infiltrate my consciousness then minute I close my eyes.

But at least I have *sevdah*. I have my mother's favorite song and Amila's favorite song to get me through the misery that is life after them. *Sevdah*-that melancholic music that seems to heal better than any doctor.

Just *sevdah*.

Vesna

The thing is, you see, I am writing this letter in hopes it never finds you. It's the only way I can force myself to be honest with you. Let me start by saying that I miss you. I still picture your smile when you'd talk about the books you read that week and I still see your hands covered in blisters from all the hard work you did. I know the last time we spoke you stood at that station waving goodbye and I spoke the biggest lie I ever told:

"I'm coming back to you".

I'm sorry I never returned your phone calls and that I never wrote back to you. I wish I had. Samira told me that you are married now. I hope she makes you happy. Samira tells me you still ask about me. She told me that several years ago you told her that you'd never fall in love again. I guess you broke your promise just like I broke mine. America is a tough country, you know. It breaks your heart in many ways. There really aren't any pots of gold to be found here. Just misery. But I finished school, like I promised I would. I have a good job now. I send money back to mama and babo every week so not much is left over. But I have to do it, anyway. They say the pensions have been cut again. That people are starving. Are you? Do you have food to eat? I worry about you, Amar.

I realize that's a loaded statement from someone that never wrote you back, but it's true. I do worry about you. Does she treat you well? I hope she does. I really do. I hope you are happy. I'm not mad at you.

They found my brother's bones. He was buried in one of the mass graves back east. I guess I'm coming home now. I get to finally bury him. He was so young, Amar. Just a boy. They say he died a painful death. His hands were clutched to that picture of us from before the war. Some nights it's like I can hear his screams. I hear all of their screams.

It's shameful that the rest of the world couldn't.

I'm scared, Amar. I'm afraid to return. I'm not that young girl you once loved effortlessly. America changed me. Or maybe it was the war that did. That bloody war. But, at least I escaped. I hurt, Amar. I hurt for our home, for what it once was, and I hurt for us.

I guess what I am trying to say is that I hope you forgive me. I'm 10 years late but I'm making good on my promise. I'm coming back to you. I'm coming home. I'm keeping my promise, Amar but I forgive you for not keeping yours. Distance and war weaken even the strongest of loves. Even ours.

Fatima

My mother never tells me about home. She says that our lives shouldn't be spent living in the past. I am a daughter of immigrant parents who refuse to admit they are immigrants. I'm not sure if they feel too afraid to tell me about home, if their wounds once opened by remembering will not be able to close. I forgive them for it. Although, I would love to know about home.

I spend hours looking at pictures of the cities, rivers, mountains, and villages belonging to a country I don't remember. It all looks beautiful. Sarajevo with its various architecture surrounded by mountains, Mostar and its old bridge, newly rebuilt, Pocitelj and its castle, Tuzla and its caves, Blagaj and its dervish house. The mosques and the churches and synagogues. One tiny country and yet so much pain seems to have hit it.

I miss it and yet I have never even seen it. I love it and yet I barely know it. I find peace in the books and stories I read about it. When I put them down, I feel loss. Immense loss. I think a part of me is somewhere in that country and so my soul feels restless until I return to retrieve that part. One day, I will return to that beautiful land that people didn't know how to appreciate.

There is that saying of "home is where the heart is" and my heart is split between two homes. Both which are greatly different from one another. A part of me is here in this country, and it's a beautiful country too, a land of opportunity and diversity. But that other part of me, the one that is in Bosnia, that's the part that hurts the most.

It's not easy to go through life missing something that you never actually had and yearning for a home that was never really yours.

My parents do not speak their native language anymore. They don't make the food that came from there. They don't listen to the music from that place. They refuse to speak the word Bosnia. My mother says we should not live in the past and yet how does one survive their future if they do not know their past. How can I feel whole if I am split in two? How can I be free if I feel trapped by the lack of knowledge of who I actually am?

My ancestors were kind people, from what I read about. They seemed to have loved all of the things a person should love; music, art, religion, and beauty in all its forms. When I read about the people that Bosnia gave birth I find myself in them. We are a melancholic people, a people that loved too much and forgave far too easily. I guess, that is why our history seems to have repeated so often. One war after another, one genocide to follow the last.

It's the genocide that my parents especially refuse to talk about. They left the year I was born, the same year the war ended. I don't know what happened to them to make them want to forget the beauty of such a country. Even if there is pain to go with it, isn't the pain sometimes worth the beauty this world offers?

We can't have one without the other, in my opinion.

They do not wish to return to their homes. They don't feel they have anything left for them there, but I think they're wrong. I think home is still home, even if it has hurt you in the past. There is always something left for us in the countries that gave us life. There are just simply pieces of us scattered in our homes that we are too afraid to return to.

I think this is what it means to be an immigrant. It means to be burdened by the memories you know you could have had in the home you left. It means to hurt every day by the fact you are separated from something you love. It means to distract yourself from your past by concerning far too much on an unknown future. It means to be broken, to be split in two, to have pieces of your being scattered across oceans, cities, and continents that you never knew. It means to be lost, forever.

To lose a home, means we lose ourselves too. Whether we want to admit it or not, this is the worst part of being an immigrant.

One day I will return to that home and I will find myself again. I'll be put together and I will be whole. Not a half human with half a soul and a heart that's split in two but rather a real person with a whole heart and soul that loves and knows two places at once.

Till then, till the day I return I have my books, my stories, my pictures of a home I never knew. I have dreams of valleys and mountains I never got to see. I have pain of loss that will carry me to return and I will. One day, I will go to my Bosnia and she will greet me with open arms and give me back that piece of my soul.

Footnotes

Saheed-   Arabic word
for martyr

Salah-   Muslim
prayer

Allah-   Arabic name
for God

Alhamdulillah-   Muslim phrase
meaning "praise be to God"

Kahva-   Bosnian word
for coffee

Kocka-   Bosnian word
for sugar cube

Kceri Moja-   daughter of
mine

Mahala-   Bosnian word
for neighborhood

Avlija-   Bosnian word
for

"Sto te nema" – Bosnian sevdah song, meaning "why are you not here"

"Zaplakala Secer Djula"- Bosnian sevdah song meaning "The Sweet Rose Wept"

"Karanfile Cvijece Moje"- Bosnian sevdah song meaning "Carnation, My Flower"

Sevdah/ Sevdalinka- traditional genre of folk music from Bosnia and Herzegovina. Sevdalinka songs are emotionally charged, melancholic, and often have an elaborate melody that invoke feelings of memory, love, and longing for the past.

Acknowledgements

To my daughter Ajsa for the happiness she brings every day to my life. To my mother and father who have always been the most supportive of all. To my friends who pushed me to write more. To my family in Bosnia who I miss every day. To my team at the Bosniak American Association of Iowa. To all the people in my life who have loved me, supported, and have shown me kindness, thank you. I am forever indebted to each of you for your love. To the country that gave birth to me.

About the Author

Arnesa Buljusmic-Kustura was born in Sarajevo, Bosnia and Herzegovina prior to the start of the war. She currently lives in Iowa where she works as a freelance writer, analyst and is in the process of obtaining her Master's Degree in Sociology. Letters from Diaspora is her first book and was inspired by the stories of war she heard from friends and strangers alike, as well as her own experiences. She is in the process of writing her second book which will be a novel.

Made in the USA
Coppell, TX
22 July 2022